The Wee Christmas Letters

CHRISTMAS MIRACLES IN THE MIDST OF WAR

MARCUS WILLIAMS

WILLIAMS & CO. PUBLISHING

WILLIAMS & Co. PUBLISHING

Contents

Chapter 1

ADELINE

My Dearest Husband,

My hands are trembling as I type this letter, and I pray my words make sense and that my tears won't smudge the ink. It has been four days since that dreadful night, and I don't know what else to do but write to you. I have nowhere to send this letter and don't even know if you are alive to read it. No, I can't talk like that. I can't lose hope, not until I know for sure.

I have been in contact with your parents in Edinburgh and they are coming out to meet me as soon as they can. I fear now that it was a mistake for us to elope and plan to surprise them when we arrived. It has certainly not turned out as we had planned. I would laugh if it all didn't feel so hopeless.

When I first sent a telegram to your parents, I didn't even get a response. It was only after my second that your father replied. At first, he accused me of instigating a cruel prank and begged me to stop for your mother's sake. They knew you were on the ship and that your name was not listed in the paper as one of the survivors. I still don't think that they believe I am your wife. Luckily, you mentioned me to them in your last letter, so at least my name was familiar to them. All of our photographs, the wedding certificate, my visa, everything went down with the ship. Well, other than my ring. At least I still have that to show them.

As I await their arrival, I have been blessed to have been taken in by the loveliest woman here in Oban. The Coast Guard brought us here instead of Glasgow, as they are stationed in the harbor here. Anyway, she and her husband are tobacconists on the high street, but he enlisted as soon as war was declared with Germany. He is currently in flight training as a bombardier, and she doesn't know if she will have the chance to see him before he is deployed to the front.

I can't believe we were so stupid as to ignore the newspapers and our friends, your uncle particularly. They warned us that Germany was targeting civilian ships, but we were convinced we would be safe. It pains me to think back on our blindness to the situation. I know now that Americans have no idea the horrors that are happening in Europe. I don't think they want to know. But they are real. I know that know.

Her name is Mildred, the woman who took me in, that is. She and her husband have been married for ten years but have no children. She is so lovely. At tea yesterday (I still can't get used to your English tea) I began to cry with no warning. That's how it seems to be these days. I try so hard to be strong, but the littlest thing reminds me of you and I just burst out in tears. Oh George, where are you? Are you all right? Please, send me a sign. Anything.

I'm sorry. My mind is like that at the moment. It jumps around and the smallest reminder throws me into despair.

I keep thinking of the day we first met, when I was walking down the sidewalk intent on getting home out of the rain, and you walked right into my path. Of course, you'll say that I walked into you. You always do. My book fell from my hands into a muddy puddle. We both bent down to pick it up, and you bumped into me so that I fell flat on my bottom into the puddle. I can laugh about it now, but oh I was so angry with you at that moment. I had just laundered my skirt the day before and it was covered in mud. But you laughed, picked up my sodden book, and grabbed me by the hand to help me up.

Your hat had fallen off of your head and you were soaked through just as I was. As soon as I saw your smile, my anger just melted away. Well, to be honest, not completely. I was still worried about the cost of replacing the book.

But then you spoke and you had that Scottish brogue I love so much. You offered to walk me home and even took the book to see if it could be saved. At the time I thought you were just being a gentleman, but now I think maybe you just wanted an excuse to see me again. In truth, I'm so glad you did. I don't know that I would have had the courage to ask you.

Anyway, Mildred, when she heard about all of the passengers rescued at sea without any belongings but the clothes on our backs, kindly offered her spare bedroom to one of the refugees. That's what they're calling us—refugees. It's silly. I don't see myself as a refugee. I was, we were, on our honeymoon. We were traveling for pleasure. I'm not like the poor Czech or Polish people who have been so brutally forced from their homes. Despite how they label me, I was lucky enough to be assigned by the local church benevolent society to Mildred's home. She has been a blessing.

For the first night, I shared the room with a young Scottish girl from Glasgow named Shelagh, but she was able to catch a bus the next day to get home. They have only allowed those who can prove residency to leave Oban thus far. I'm not sure where that leaves me.

I apologize; Mildred just called me down to tea. I don't know what I would do without her. She is like my rock, the only steady thing in my life right now. Does that sound silly? We've only known each other for a few days, yet I feel like we have known each other forever. She has become such a dear friend.

That night replays in my head over and over. I can't seem to make it stop, like I'm at the pictures and the film is broken and just replaying the same scene again and again. We were so happy. Our journey was almost at an end. We were going to meet your parents and surprise them with the news of our marriage. And then the whistle sounded and the horn blared, and chaos, just chaos descended upon the ship.

I'm grateful we were walking up on the deck instead of in our cabin. They say it was a German torpedo that hit us. Did you know that? Why would they have attacked us? We were just a passenger ship. We were no threat to them. I'll never forget the screaming noise of the torpedo right before the night exploded. You caught me when the deck buckled from the explosion. I was screaming, but you kept your head. I don't know how you did, but I can see the steely determination on your face as you almost had to drag me to the nearest lifeboat. I was in a panic and couldn't seem to force my legs to move. It was only you propelling me forward that got me there.

Why oh why didn't you join me in the boat? We were one of the first to arrive and there was plenty of room. But of course you didn't. You thought more of the women and children than yourself, and that is one of the reasons I love you. On one hand I wouldn't have it any other way, yet I so desperately wish that for once you would have been selfish and stayed by my side.

No, that isn't true. I would never want you to stop helping others. It's just my grief talking.

Do you remember that day last spring? It seems like so long ago now, but it was only this past May. We were walking together in the park, talking about what a future together would be like and how it would work. My father needs constant care. His wounds from the Great War are so much deeper than the scars on his legs. My mother passed away two years ago now. How could I leave him alone to be with you? And your family, your future, they are here in Scotland. There was that squirrel in the big oak tree in the park who was chittering away over the park bench where we sat. I had almost given up hope completely that we could ever be together. It looked like it was going to be the end, right then and there, when that squirrel dropped an acorn right on my head. Just like that.

It hurt like the dickens, but it knocked sense into me, didn't it? It was like that little squirrel was listening to all of my defeatist talk and wanted me to snap out of it. No sooner did I regain my senses that you dropped to one knee to propose, like you were in league with the squirrel! Maybe it should have been your best man. Haha. Poor you. You had such big plans for a romantic stroll in the park and a happy engagement, and I almost ruined it all by breaking up with you. I can laugh about it now. I hope you can too. It's definitely a story we will tell our grandchildren one day.

Oh, my dearest George. You have to be alive. You just have to. How will we tell our grandchildren about the day we were engaged if you've left me? We have so many plans.

I was able to send a telegram to my father to let him know that I survived the attack, but I couldn't bring myself to tell him that you are, what word should I use? I can't give up hope. Not yet. Not so close to Christmas. Lost? Is that the right word?

I was so excited to experience some of your Christmas traditions with your family. I don't know how we will carry on with them if you aren't here. It just won't be the same. I'm sure your parents feel that way too. Will they accept me? You always promised me that they would just love me, but now that this has happened, I'm terrified that they will blame me or only feel your absence whenever they look at me.

I know that's not rational. Mildred has told me over and over that it isn't my fault, but I can't help but think that I should have insisted that you join me in the boat. Maybe if I had been more hysterical, you would have joined me to comfort me. But I was trying to be brave, show you that I was strong. As the lifeboat was lowered to the sea and we motored away, I watched for you on the deck, but I lost you in the melee of people trying to escape. I searched for you until my eyes hurt from the strain. And finally, when the ship slipped below the surface, I screamed that we had to go back and search for you and others who may have been thrown into the sea.

I pleaded with the sailor manning our lifeboat. I cried. I yelled. I'm afraid I made quite a scene. But I didn't care. All I could think about was you floating in the ice cold water, just waiting for me to come back for you. Do you blame me for not coming back? Should I have tried harder? The other passengers almost had to restrain me as it was. I think I scared them actually. But I don't care.

That first night on the ship... I'm sitting here with tears streaming down my cheeks but laughing at the same time at the memory. It was only because your stomach started grumbling so loudly that we even realized it was dinner time. We hurriedly got ready and raced to the dining room, where apparently everyone had been waiting for us to make an entrance. I guess word had spread that we were on our honeymoon. Everyone began laughing and cheering when we entered the room, all disheveled from having gotten ready so quickly. I'm sure we were a sight. I could tell my cheeks had turned bright red; they were so hot with embarrassment.

But you took it all in stride and waved to the crowd with a big grin. You even bowed, much to their amusement. The crowd erupted in hoots and hollers—most undignified. The maitre d led us to the Captain's table where we were his guests of honor for the evening. I was mortified! But at the same time, I was so proud that you were mine and only mine. Forever. The other women in the room burned with jealousy, I could tell.

I don't care if the priest said, "till death do us part." You are my love now and always. You must be. How will I survive otherwise?

Evening has fallen and we are under strict black out orders, so I must switch off the desk lamp now. I'm sure

I will fold this letter and place it in an envelope as if I fully intend to drop it in the post tomorrow. But I know not where to send it. Should I instead seal it in a bottle and cast it into the sea?

Oh, George, just send me a sign. Anything.

Your loving wife,

Adeline

P.S. I read over the letter and fear I may have rambled on a bit. I'm sorry for that. But I must say once again that I love you more than life itself. Come back to me.

Chapter 2

GEORGE

Darling Adeline,

I awoke this morning to learn that I have been sleeping for four days. I believe that I scared the nurse when I tried to get out of bed and get dressed. I am so weak that I collapsed back into bed. I had to ask her where I am, and my heart dropped when she told me I am at the clinic in Castlebay on the Isle of Barra in the Outer Hebrides.

I was so confused, but the nurse called the doctor who explained to me what happened and how I got here. Between you and me, I'm not sure if he is even a real doctor. He was a medic during the Great War and apparently was the only person with medical training on the island, which made him the de facto doctor. I heard him giving medical advice on a sheep to a patient in the next bed. It's possible he knows more about animals than humans.

My memory is slowly returning in bits and pieces, and the more I recall, the more worried I become. The nurse has warned me more than once that I am getting myself into a state, and my blood pressure is too high. I can't argue with her there. I constantly feel on the edge of panic.

I do recall bits and pieces of our final dinner on the ship. You were absolutely stunning in your midnight blue gown. I can remember the man across from us at the table (an American I think?) talking about going to Scotland to sell some sort of engine part that can be used in military vehicles. It is such a random thing to remember, I know. I don't remember everything he said, but can clearly remember that you did not like the man.

And there was the talk of German U-boats. Did the captain make an announcement or was it just talk amongst the passengers? It seems like someone told us that as we sailed closer to the coast, we were at much higher risk of attack, that U-boats had been reported in the area. Am I remembering correctly?

"Make sure you keep your life vests close," I recall someone saying. Was that you my darling?

It is so frustrating to not be able to see things clearly. I feel as though I am drowning in fog.

I do have a picture in my mind of you in the lifeboat being lowered to the sea, and I am grateful for that. I pray that your life was spared and that you were rescued by the coast guard.

I had to take a break from writing and rest. I injured my head somehow, and the doctor said it is the cause of my memory issues. It's wrapped in a bandage and begins to throb whenever I try to focus on the words I am writing. But I am determined to finish my letter to you. You must be worried sick.

I hope that you have been able to connect with my parents.

A fisherman came in to visit me this afternoon. I guess word has spread throughout the village that I finally woke up. He spoke mostly Gaelic, but between what I remember from school and his broken English, I was able to piece together what happened.

He said that he and his brother were preparing to launch their boat when they heard the distress signal over the radio. They rushed out to sea to help. When they arrived, the coast guard was already there taking aboard the passengers from the lifeboats, so they searched the debris for any survivors and found me, unconscious, my arm wrapped around a life preserver. By the time they managed to pull me aboard, the coast guard cutter had already left, so they brought me home to the clinic on Barra.

Why didn't I get into the lifeboat with you? Do you remember? What happened afterwards? How did I get this head injury? I can't answer any of those questions. It's just a blank space in my memory.

I do remember you reaching for my hand under the table at dinner and squeezing three times, our secret little way of saying "I love you." Just a small thing, but that feeling in my hand buoys me up in this difficult time.

I'm so sorry to have left you alone in a strange country, especially for the fact that you will have to meet my parents without me at your side and explain to them that we have already been married. It was such a fun idea at the time, wasn't it? The paperwork, your visa, our wedding certificate, are all now at the bottom of the sea.

I don't even know where you are. I refuse to even consider the possibility that you didn't make it. I cling with every ounce of faith I can muster to that memory of you on the lifeboat. You must have survived! But where are you now? Are they taking good care of you? Do you have someplace warm to sleep?

The nurse just came in again to check my blood pressure and change the dressing on my head wound. She made me promise to wrap up this letter soon or she said she would take away the pen and paper.

I asked the fisherman who saved my life if he could take me to the mainland. He said that because of the attack, the Coast Guard has issued an order forbidding any commercial or pleasure craft from leaving port until they can find and destroy the submarine that attacked us. He couldn't tell me how long that would take. It could be days or weeks. It's possible the submarine is long gone already.

I asked about sending a radio call to whomever is organizing relief efforts to get a message to you that I am alive. He said his cousin is the island's radio operator, and he is stuck in Oban where he went to get a part to repair the radio. So, the radio doesn't work, and the operator and replacement part are probably closer to you than they are to me.

It all feels so hopeless. Every time I try to get out of bed, waves of dizziness wash over me. I can't sail to you; I can't radio to you. I can't even post this letter to you.

The nurse just peeked her head in and gave me a five-minute warning.

So, I'll close with a happier memory from a happier time even if that time seems so long ago now. Did you know that when we bumped into each other, it wasn't the first time I had seen you? Are you surprised? Shocked? Well, you should be. I had no shame.

Anyway, you had passed by me every day for a week without ever seeing me; your nose was always buried in that book. I tried to muster up the courage to say something to you, but every time you passed by, my brain just froze, and I couldn't seem to remember what I had planned on saying. That day in the rain, it was like I was pushed from behind. I was standing there, once again telling myself I would at least say hello, when suddenly I was pushed right out in front of you. You ran into me, and your book fell into the puddle. Just like that, the spell that had been holding my tongue captive just vanished, and I was able to speak.

I'll never know who or what pushed me, but I will always be forever grateful. I suspect maybe an angel was sent to answer my prayers, although I don't know if I believe that's even possible. Maybe now I do. I should have never survived being in those icy waters for so long. The doctor has told me repeatedly that it is a miracle I survived.

The nurse is approaching with a steely look on her face, determined to steal away my pen so that I will rest. So, I bid you farewell, my love.

George

Chapter 3

ADELINE

Dear George,

An entire week has passed since my last letter, and I know as little now as I did a week ago. I am still living with Mildred in Oban. The people here are so lovely and Mildred has become like the sister I never had.

Did I ever tell you about the Christmas when I was eight years old? My mother had gotten pregnant twice after I was born, but both times she lost the baby. It was so hard on her. She always tried to remain cheerful and happy for me, but I heard her crying in the bathroom when she thought I wasn't listening. She never once made me feel like it was a disappointment to her to only have me. I will never be able to comprehend her strength. I didn't understand it until I was an adult and read her diary from that time in her life.

Anyway, I'm rambling. Even though the days are short (it gets dark by mid-afternoon) they still feel long to me. I am stuck here in limbo.

So, back to my story. I was eight years old and desperate for a little sister to play with. My best friend Betty came from a family of six children and I loved going to her house. I loved the noise and the chaos of children running around and hanging on their mother's skirt. I decided that I would write a letter to Santa Claus to ask for a new baby sister. I sat at the kitchen table for hours composing the perfect letter outlining how I would be the best big sister ever. I used my best penmanship. When I finished, I asked my mother for an envelope and a stamp. She told me that letters to Santa did not require a stamp, so I bundled up and walked in the snow down to the corner mailbox where I dropped in the letter.

On Christmas morning I ran downstairs fully expecting, as only a child could, that a little baby would be lying under the tree wrapped in a little Christmas blanket and sucking her thumb. Boy was I disappointed. I dropped to my knees on the floor and just stared at the tree. When my parents came downstairs, my mother kindly took me by the shoulders and led me to the couch where she set a gift in my lap. As you might have guessed, the gift was the most beautiful doll I had ever seen. But in the moment, I cast it aside and ran up to my room and slammed the door.

It embarrasses me to tell this story now. When the depression hit, there wasn't enough for even a doll under the tree on Christmas. I should have been grateful for what I had. Years later, I was in the attic going through some of my mother's things, and I found my letter to Santa tucked away in a corner next to that little doll. I just broke into sobs. Santa must have returned it to her. I couldn't believe how insensitive I had been. There I was asking Santa Claus for a baby, not realizing how it hurt my mother's feelings. I can't imagine how difficult it would have been for her to buy me that doll when she so desperately wanted to give me the baby sister I asked for.

Maybe Mildred is the answer to my childhood Christmas wish! I may finally have the sister I always wished for.

I have begun to help her in the shop during the day. She wanted to pay me for my work, but I refused. I owe her already for the room and board and especially for her friendship. I don't believe I can legally work anyway given my refugee status. There's that word again.

The last I heard, the consulate in Glasgow has reached out to the Immigration Service in London to verify my visa status. They have also written to the county courthouse back home to get a copy of our marriage license. I am essentially having to redo all of the paperwork by mail. I tried to explain that we were only visiting and planned to return to the States, but they said that as you are of fighting age and a UK citizen, you fall under the National Service Act. There is a slim chance that because of your occupation and your company's trade with the United States, that you might be exempt. But you still have to register.

Of course, none of that matters now. Right now, all I care about is that you are out there somewhere, alive and trying to get to me.

It's funny that we never thought that you might not be able to return to the States after coming here. Maybe you did, but it never even crossed my mind. I mean, I know that you are from Scotland of course, but I just saw you as the man I met and fell in love with back home. It was silly of me of course.

I heard from your parents. Your mother wrote me a very kind letter. The tone was a bit formal but that might just be a cultural difference. You did say your mother can be, how did you word it, straight-laced. Is that the word you used? It doesn't seem quite right. Although you promised that she would warm to me when she got to know me, I'm afraid the barrier between us is much higher now without you here. She didn't come out and say that she blames me but I can read between the lines. I keep telling myself it is just her grief talking.

She explained that your father has to wrap up an important contract and then they have to secure a train ticket to Glasgow and catch the bus to Oban. I thought that you said they own an automobile, so I don't quite understand why they are taking the train instead of driving but I'm sure they have a reason. She estimates that they will be able to get to Oban by next week at the latest. She wrote that she is excited to meet me and even said she is sure I am lovely because her son has excellent taste. However, I still sense a bit of hesitation in her willingness to see me as her daughter-in-law. I'm sure it will just take time.

I wonder if you've ever been to Oban. The city is truly magical. Mildred and her husband live in the apartment above their shop, so it is very convenient getting to work each day. Yesterday I realized that I hadn't left the building for three days. Can you believe that? I went from the upstairs apartment to the shop downstairs and back without any reason to go outside, so I never did.

You know how much I love being outdoors. I have been in such a daze that I never even considered that I should be getting out. When customers come into the shop, I try to smile and be helpful. Some of them ask about America, but most give me a look of pity and hurry on their way. I think they just don't really know what to say to me. I'm still no good at counting out the money here, so Mildred keeps me busy stocking shelves and taking inventory.

Yesterday I was feeling particularly down as I was organizing the magazine shelf. Mildred caught me staring at the cover of a magazine. She said I had a blank look on my face that reminded her of the look she had seen in the faces of veterans from the Great War. My mind was in a faraway place, with you wherever you are. So, she took the magazine from my hand, helped me into a coat, and shooed me out the door. She ordered me to walk along the harbor road as far as the kirk and back and said she wouldn't let me back inside until I had.

It was exactly what I needed. I walked across the lane and then along the waterfront. The harbor is full of fishing vessels. I've been told that the Coast Guard has ordered them to stay in port until they finish searching for the German U-Boat. Even though they aren't allowed to go out and fish, the docks were teeming with fishermen working on their boats and catching up with maintenance.

I waved at one man when he looked up from detangling a fishing net and caught me watching. He smiled and waved back and then his companion looked up and whistled at me. It has happened to me before of course. In the past I always found it flattering, if not a bit crass. I never knew how to react, but it was different this time because of you.

Remember that time when we were walking home from the cinema and I forgot my gloves, so you ran back inside to get them? I waited outside of the theater while you asked the usher to let you back in. I watched the other couples as they walked hand in hand down the street or got into their automobiles. You know I find it fascinating just to watch people. Anyway, as you came out of the door with my gloves in hand, a car stopped at the intersection and the passenger leaned out of his window and whistled at me. Instead of getting angry at him and yelling like other men would have, you took me in your arms, dipped me like we were Fred and Ginger, and kissed me in front of everyone! I turned bright red, I'm sure, but the man in the car laughed and congratulated you before his companion drove away.

How did I get so lucky? I just pray that my luck hasn't run out and that you are still out there trying to find me.

Back to my story. The young man on the docks whistled, but I just smiled and held up my hand to show him my ring. He made an exaggerated groan and his friend slapped him on the back in consolation. It was all good natured and in good fun.

I continued walking along the harbor path until I reached the kirk. I stepped inside, but there was a group of people talking up near the altar, so I quietly said a little prayer for you and then left. As I prayed, a feeling of peace washed over me which I honestly find hard to explain. I tried to tell myself that it meant you are alive and well, but that didn't feel right. Instead, the thought came to me that all would be well no matter what happened. I'm not sure I like that answer but I must admit that it brings me comfort.

I realized that I desperately needed that moment of peace in my life. In my cries to God to bring you back to me, I am embarrassed to admit that I have failed to show my gratitude for everything I do have. Even if we are never reunited, which is something I still can't bear to think about, I will always be grateful for the time we have had together.

I left the church and decided to keep walking. The rain had stopped, and the fresh air, combined with my experience in the church, had revived my spirits. Further down the path was a small grassy area with a park bench looking out over the harbor. It has the most beautiful view of the bay and the lighthouse on the island across the water. In the park there is a faded sign that tells the story of Fingal's Dog Stone just up ahead between the park and Dunollie Castle. The legend says that the stone is where the ancient Celtic hero Fingal would chain his massive dog, Bran.

There is a groove around the bottom where Bran's chain wore down the stone. They say you can hear the dog's ghost howling at night. I hope never to experience that phenomenon! But I just love the history here.

I decided to walk as far as the base of the hill where the castle is located before I turned back. Maybe next time I will walk up the hill to explore the castle.

As I sit here at the typewriter, my mind is flooded with things I want to tell you. I want you to know everything about me. I want to share every experience from my childhood and hear all of your stories growing up in this magical place. I know you grew up in Edinburgh, but I imagine it is just as magical as Oban.

I am running out of ribbon on the typewriter, which is a sign it is time for me to close this letter. I've decided I would end it by telling you one of the reasons that I love you.

You probably don't even remember this, but it sticks out in my mind. When we were boarding the ship, there was a young woman who was struggling to carry her bag while balancing a crying toddler on her hip. I could see she was very frustrated, and I approached her to ask if I could help. She told me that she was fine and thanked me for offering, so I smiled and turned to leave.

But not you. You didn't ask her if she needed help. You could see that she did. So instead of walking away, you gently took the bag from her shoulder and told her you would carry it for her to her cabin. She made a small effort to protest, but she was so grateful for your help and kindness. But that's who you are. You just stepped in.

Did you know that she found me one day during the voyage? Well, she did. I was reading in the lounge and she rushed up to me and just gushed at how lucky I am. I laughed and agreed with her, but she became very serious. A tear trickled down her cheek and she took me by the shoulders and made me swear that I would never let you go. We sat and talked and she told me horror stories about her husband's fondness for drink and his foul temper. She was right, you know, I am lucky to have found you.

Now, if only I can find you again. It is my only Christmas wish.

I love you.

Adeline

Chapter 4

GEORGE

My Dearest Adeline,

Would you like to hear something silly? This morning when I woke up, I asked the nurse if there was a letter from you in the post. It didn't even cross my mind that you have no idea where I am and there is no post as long as the boats are all still in port. For some reason I woke up this morning thinking I was just away on a business trip or something. It must have been a dream.

Unfortunately, the nurse did not find my question amusing and called for the doctor to reassess my head wound. He asked me if I knew the names of the British king and the American president. He shone a little pen light in my eyes. I kept trying to convince him that I'm much better now and that it was just a dream. And in truth, I am feeling much better. My head only hurts if I am subjected to bright light, of which there is very little on this perpetually cloudy island.

They feed me well and I have regained my strength. One of the local women brings in freshly baked bread and either lamb stew or fish. Another patient in the hospital said the fish would be much better if the fishermen were allowed to go out. It all tastes wonderful to me, even if it is a bit repetitive.

I do notice one difference however, but I'm not sure if it is because of the accident or because I have been away from Scotland for so long. I constantly have a chill. The dampness in the air seems to seep through my clothing. I've heard foreigners say the same thing when they visit Scotland, but as a native I thought I was immune to the Scottish weather. Perhaps floating in the icy sea for so long had a negative effect.

I am allowed to go out for a walk around Castlebay every afternoon. The small charity shop in town donated a wool sweater and knit cap for me to wear. I still have the coat I was wearing when our ship went down.

I spend ten minutes every morning running through the events of the last day on the ship through my mind to try and get my memory back. The doctor told me that my efforts will be in vain, that the brain doesn't work that way. But I have little else to do, so I still try. I still remember almost nothing after my last picture of you being lowered in the lifeboat. Even that is more like a photograph than a memory.

The little village here is beautiful, and I find peace walking through the streets. There is a church on the hill overlooking the bay. I generally step into the church to offer a prayer for your safety. Honestly, it is more like I am begging God that we may be reunited soon. Just thinking about how worried you must be is painful to me. If only I could contact you somehow. I'm not certain I am worthy of having my prayers answered, but you certainly are my love, so I lean on the hope that He will answer them for your sake if not for mine.

This afternoon I went to the post office to ask if I could make a call to the mainland from the local phone box. Much to my dismay, he told me the lines had been cut and they had no idea when they would be repaired. I feel as deserted as Robinson Crusoe. It's the year 1939 and I have no way to communicate with anyone off the island.

I thought that I could slip into the pub without my doctor finding out, but lo and behold he was sitting at the bar when I walked in. He frowned and forbad me from drinking any alcohol, but he didn't force me to leave. The men were warm and welcoming. A cozy peat fire burned in the hearth, and just like a picture postcard, a dog slept on the rug in front of the fire. All of the people in the pub seem to have family or friends on the mainland that they are trying to contact. We are currently in the dark about the status of the war or the news in general. Since the night of the attack almost two weeks ago, the entire island has been isolated.

I met a fisherman at the pub who reminded me of a friend from university in Stirling. I don't think I've told you about him. I was of course there to study business so that I could work for my father when I graduated. My friend Ian was studying theology. Despite our very different coursework, we met when we both tried out for the university football club. I had gotten it in my head that I was a good enough footballer to play at that level, but was quickly disabused of that notion. Ian, on the other hand, was brilliant and made the team.

Anyway, we struck up a friendship and spent a lot of time together. He introduced me to the first girl that I ever dated and we spent hours debating and discussing anything and everything we could think of. I remember one Saturday night in particular. We were in a pub very similar to the one here and we were debating the reality of love at first sight.

Are you surprised that two college lads would engage in such a discussion over a pint on a Saturday night? Well, maybe we were different from our mates, but we had those types of discussions often.

You must be wondering what position I took in the debate. You may be surprised to know that I argued against the theory of love at first sight. In fact, I argued that, although attraction is real, love can only grow over time. Oh, how I was wrong! Much to my surprise, I quickly changed my mind the very first time that I saw you walking down the street. I couldn't focus on anything else. My work suffered. I couldn't eat. I finally understood what the phrase meant. I honestly don't know how my love for you could grow any deeper. I think if it does, I will burst.

Ian, on the other hand, was convinced that he would know the woman he was going to marry the moment he saw her. In a twist of fate, he has been dating the same girl for a year now and we met and married within months.

I apologize, my love. I've been rambling. I just want to tell you everything about me and am worried now that I'll never get the chance. What if this war never ends and we are effectively quarantined here forever? At times, this island feels like a prison. I swear that I will be true to you, no matter what happens.

But back to the discussion in the pub. The men were plotting and planning ways to somehow communicate with the mainland without being caught by the Coast Guard. It's not just that they are afraid of repercussions from violating the order, they genuinely don't want to distract them from their duties searching for the U-Boat. One of the men said that he has a small boat that he could sail along the coast up to Eoligarry on the northern side of the island and then make a run for the Isle of South Uist. Many of the others argued that his boat was too small to take that far out from the coast. The seas can be very dangerous and unpredictable, especially this time of year. I think they finally convinced him that it is too dangerous, and the restrictions would end soon anyway, but it is an option if things don't change. There is a radio operator in Lochboisdale on South Uist who may be able to get word to Oban.

The local innkeeper was also there at the pub. His name is Alasdair. He was talking about the restrictions and happened to mention that a Coast Guard ship came into Castlebay just days after the attack, but no one thought to inform the crew that I had been rescued and was lying in the hospital just down the lane. They could have then easily gotten word to the crew in Oban. But they departed and I was still lying unconscious. In their defense, they didn't yet know my name, but they could have at least given my description to the crew.

When Alasdair made the comment, it didn't even cross his mind how it would impact me, so I don't blame him. But my heart sank into my gut. If just one person had thought to mention me, you would know that I survived.

I guess I went suddenly pale because the doctor noticed the look on my face and ordered me to immediately return to the hospital to rest. He wouldn't even allow me to walk, although it is only a five-minute walk at most.

I spent the rest of that evening in a daze, torturing myself over what could have been or should have been. Since then, I have realized that wishing things had been done differently is not helpful. What is the American expression? "No use crying over spilt milk," I think it is. What's done is done. I can only look forward from here.

I don't think it is fair that I continue to occupy a bed at the hospital now that I am feeling better. I am getting restless. I know I should still rest and take it easy, but I need to do something. The people have been so kind to me; I must repay them somehow. I plan to ask around in the next few days. Maybe someone could use help with their business accounting or management. I don't know who or what it would be, but I could trade my skills for room and board at least. There is a fishery on the island that delivers to the mainland. Maybe they could use my help.

Although I know nothing of sheep herding, I am even willing to learn that if that is what is needed. I can follow instructions well enough. I must at least earn my keep. I am choosing to trust that the restrictions will lift soon and that the weather will cooperate so that we may be reunited.

I promise that I will do everything in my power to hold you in my arms by Christmas. Stay strong, my love.

George

Chapter 5

ADELINE

My Darling George,

Your parents arrived yesterday evening, and I would love to say that they are wonderful. I'm sure they are; they raised a wonderful son after all. But it was a difficult evening. Maybe they were just tired from their long journey. I know they are grieving just as I am. Sometimes I forget that I am not the only one who loves you and is frantically worried about you. Every day that passes without knowing what happened to you feels like another weight dragging me down with the ship.

They explained why they couldn't drive here. Because of the war, petrol is scarce and being rationed, which makes sense. So, they took the train to Glasgow and the bus to Oban.

As we sat in Mildred's small living room and spent time talking and getting to know each other, your father became very short when your mother started talking about seeing you again.

"His ship went down in the North Atlantic," he said. "Even if he survived the sinking, he wouldn't have lasted more than a few minutes in the water." He said it with such certainty and coldness that I was shocked. Your mother sobbed and ran from the room. His shoulders slumped and he looked so empty and hopeless at that moment. But in a flash, he shook his head and forced a smile before he turned his attention back to me. As if we were simply two people getting to know each other, he asked me to tell him about where I grew up, where I went to school, and other just, normal things, as if our situation isn't an extraordinary one.

After I suffered through a few minutes of awkward conversation with your father, your mother came back into the room, her tears wiped away and her makeup reapplied. They didn't speak of you again, which was so hard for me. All I wanted to do was ask them about you and hear stories about your childhood. I so desperately hoped meeting them would help me feel closer to you. But if anything, they seem to be keeping their grief at arm's length.

When my mother died, all of us were so lost, but her funeral was such a special time for me. I'll never forget it. My Uncle Charlie gathered us around and spent hours telling us stories about my mother's childhood—how he teased her relentlessly, and how she always got him back in the end. We laughed and cried so hard together that afternoon.

I remember one story in particular that made me laugh. My mom was probably eight or nine years old and Charlie, who was six years older, decided to trick her into thinking her favorite doll had run away. He put all of her doll clothes on her bed and made sure a few outfits were missing. He then wrote a note from the doll to my mom in childish handwriting and left it next to the pile of clothes. It said something like, "I am running away to become a real girl. Please don't search for me. Love, Cindy." That was her doll's name. Anyway, my mom searched the entire house for Cindy and couldn't find her. She was distraught.

She went crying to her mom, my grandmother, who suggested that she check to see if Cindy had just gone outside. Sure enough, my mom searched in all of the outbuildings and found Cindy sitting in the outhouse with the Saturday Evening Post propped in her arms and her little drawers around her ankles. My mom grabbed Cindy up and turned to find Charlie laughing hysterically at her. Charlie said my mom just gave him the evil eye and stormed back into the house. She waited patiently for the perfect moment to exact her revenge.

It was almost a year later when she learned that Charlie was falling in love with a girl from Sunday School—his first love. My mom wrote a letter to the girl, I forget her name, in Charlie's handwriting in which "he" confessed his undying love for her and promised to do the girl's chores for her for the rest of the school year. Charlie was so confused when the girl smiled at him the next day and handed him a list of chores, all of which he said were too "girly" for a boy to do. He was so mad when he found out what my mom had done! But she just told him it was payback for Cindy and they were now even.

With your parents, I felt like I was walking on eggshells. We weren't allowed to talk about you at all. The worst part was when your father spoke about putting all of your affairs in order. I so desperately wanted to scream, "We can't give up hope! Not at Christmas!"

Your parents are staying at the Inn down the road. I should be in bed now, but I couldn't sleep. I feel so much closer to you when I'm writing. I'm typing by candlelight since we are in a black out.

I believe that your parents have accepted that we are married at least. Your mother asked about the wedding. I could tell she was hurt that we eloped, so I tried to explain why we felt it important to get married so quickly. I couldn't stand to wait even one more day to be with you. I couldn't tell what your father was thinking. He made a comment about your inheritance, and I got the feeling he doesn't feel like I deserve to have it.

I tried to tell him that money isn't what is important to me; you are. I don't care about money. I didn't even know that you have an inheritance. I mean, I know that you work for your father and that the business is successful, but we haven't really ever talked about money. We had all the time in the world to talk about those kinds of things. Or at least we thought we did.

I just read through my letter and am appalled. I sound like I have started to come to terms with the fact that I may have lost you forever that night. I want to assure you that couldn't be further from the truth. I make it a point to visit the kirk every day to light a candle and say a prayer for you. It brings me some peace. It's difficult to explain, but after I pray, I feel certain that my last memory of you will not be looking up at the deck of the sinking ship as my lifeboat drifted away. I just know in my heart that that's not the end of it.

Of course, then I return home (I've started to call Mildred's place home) and lie in bed at night and the feeling of loneliness and loss almost overwhelms me. Yesterday morning, Mildred gave me a hug when I came down for tea and confessed she could hear me crying through the walls. It is such a struggle to hold out hope. The darkness creeps in when I least expect it.

Yesterday, a woman came into the shop. When I asked if I could help her, she told me that she was there to talk with me. You can imagine how confused I was. I brought her upstairs where we could talk in private. She told me how her cousin is the radio operator on one of the islands and that he had been in town to buy parts when the attack happened and the restrictions were put in place.

She said that her cousin has an old army mate whose son is a pilot for the Auxiliary Air Force out of Glasgow. Her cousin reached out to the pilot, who has agreed that the next time he is assigned to patrol the North Atlantic, he will try to reach someone on the islands by radio. If the pilot is able to contact someone, that person may be able to relay the message until it reaches all of the inhabited islands. He knows they must be starving for news. They can then send messages back the next time they see him flying overhead.

Her cousin said it's a long shot, but when he told her of his plans, she remembered my story and came by to see if there was any message I wanted to have relayed out to the islands.

Of course, I started to cry. You've married an emotional mess! But eventually I was able to speak and asked her to put out your description. Maybe someone has news of your fate. Maybe someone saw you or knows where you are. I've heard rumors that there are other survivors out there, but that may just be people hoping, people like me.

If the weather is clear, there should be a patrol flight soon. I pray this crazy plan will work. What if you are out there just waiting to tell me that you are okay and trying to make it back to me? One can hope!

I will face the dilemma of trying to convince your parents to stay in Oban for a bit longer. I have a feeling that they want to return home right away and, of course, take me with them. I will somehow have to explain to them how I feel so strongly that I must wait here until at least Christmas Day. Miracles can happen on Christmas. I truly believe that.

I am relieved that something is happening at last. Someone is willing to help me look for you.

Stay strong. Be well. Know that I love you.

Your loving bride,

Adeline

Chapter 6

GEORGE

Adeline,

I am finally out of the hospital and feeling much better. I moved in with the man I told you about last time who has the small boat. His name is Hamish MacNeil and he lives in a little cottage that has been in his family for generations. I've learned that the Isle of Barra was home to the MacNeil clan, who were known as seafaring raiders. The clan castle is out in the middle of the bay, which explains why the village is called Castlebay. It is in some disrepair, but the castle still stands sentinel over the town. I wonder how well it would stand up to a German torpedo.

Hamish is actually a carpenter by trade, but like most of the people on the island, he has been a sailor his entire life as well. The sea is just a part of life here. His little boat, more of a skiff really, is much smaller than the fishing vessels, and he believes he could avoid both the Coast Guard and the Germans if he made a run to South Uist. The biggest worry is the sea. It can be very rough this time of year and no place for such a small vessel.

Most of the others in town think Hamish's idea is a crazy one, but as more time passes without any contact with the mainland, I would venture to guess that they will be more willing to support his proposal to sail to South Uist to try and find a working radio.

In the meantime, I've been helping Hamish with his work. I'm not much of a carpenter, but I can manage some simple tasks. If all else fails, I'm handy with a broom. Honestly, I'm not helping him much, but he puts up with me in the shop and we enjoy each other's company.

Yesterday I think I was getting a bit underfoot, so he tasked me with painting some of the toys that he has made throughout the year for the local children for Christmas. He has an entire trunk full of them. Did you know that I took an art class at school? I don't think I ever told you that.

I believe I was twelve or thirteen. I broke my leg playing football on a muddy pitch, so the headmaster assigned me to spend my convalescence in art class. I had never tried my hand at painting before and was surprised at how much I enjoyed it. I spent hours that year painting the old school buildings and grounds. My instructor even said I had a future if I was willing to work hard and pursue it. I actually considered it for a moment until I thought about how that conversation would go with my father. I dropped that idea immediately. I didn't want to be an artist that badly.

It's not that my father doesn't want me to be happy. It's just that his language is business and money. He doesn't understand the arts. He would rather be examining a ledger than walking through a museum.

In fact, only a few years ago now, the Society of Scottish Artists brought an exhibit featuring Dali and Picasso to Edinburgh. Mother and I dragged my father to the exhibit after dinner one evening without telling him of our destination. I think the best part of the evening was listening to him prattling on about how ridiculous it was that people spent good money on such modern drivel. He was speechless when I told him how much the paintings were actually worth. It defied his comprehension. We had such a laugh on the way home; he went on and on about it. I think we got more entertainment from father than we did from the paintings.

Painting toys for Hamish isn't exactly the same as trying my hand at impressionist Scottish landscapes, but it has been nice to pick up a brush again. I feel an inspiration that I've missed for so many years. Tomorrow, I am going to try my hand at painting your portrait. I'm afraid I will never be able to do your beauty justice, but I certainly don't need a photograph to copy. When I close my eyes, I can see you sitting there posing for me as clear as day. I feel almost compelled to give it a try.

Hamish said he knows where we can get a blank canvas, and he already has the paints. So, I am going to give it a go. I haven't felt the inspiration to paint since my school days. Isn't it strange? If this hadn't happened to us, if we weren't living this tragedy, I probably would have never felt the desire to paint again. God truly does work in mysterious ways.

⸺

It's been a few days now since I've had the chance to write. Much has happened. I've been so focused on the painting, that the days have flown by. It helps me feel close to you when I paint. I can't say it's a masterpiece, but I must admit I am particularly fond of how I've been able to capture the hint of a smile in your eyes. It reminds me of our first proper date when we went to that little diner. Do you remember that night?

We had the table near the window and watched as people rushed by on the sidewalk outside. Our conversation was probably mundane to anyone else listening in, but to me it was captivating. I hung on your every word. So much so, that you decided to play a little joke on me and tell me a bit of a tall tale. I didn't even flinch when you started describing the troll who lived under the bridge near your childhood home. How long did you keep the story going whilst I nodded and took in every detail? You had a twinkle in your eye that just captured my attention. It wasn't until you finally broke into laughter that I realized you had been teasing me all along. That mischievous side of you—it captured my heart. I probably would have believed you if you had told me that you descended from Highland faeries.

On a more serious note, the others in town have finally agreed to let Hamish attempt the journey. The forecast is for calm seas for the next few days, so it's now or never. I have volunteered to go with him. I can't just sit here while he risks his life to help me.

I have some sailing experience, but nothing that would prepare me for sailing a small boat in the North Atlantic. Hamish and I have spent every evening for the last few days in the bay so that I may practice a little at least. If nothing else, I can provide extra muscle and follow simple orders. The plan is to drive the boat up to the north side of Barra and launch in Bágh Thiarabhagh. From there, we can hide along the coasts of smaller islands past Eriskay up to Lochboisdale. The journey, if all goes well, should take a few hours at most.

We leave this afternoon as soon as it grows dark. Wish me luck, darling. I will finish this letter once I arrive in Lochboisdale.

What an adventure that was! The sun is just coming up and I am huddled under a blanket with a cup of hot tea, trying to stop shivering. The night was so cold. The wind whipped up sea spray, drenching us in our little boat. My arms feel numb with exhaustion from the endless work during the journey. We hadn't a moment of respite the entire night.

The journey started out well enough. The seas were calm in the bay when we launched the boat. We carried an extra can of petrol for the small motor and some other supplies, but the boat isn't big enough for much else. The seas were fine as long as we sailed close to land, but as soon as we had to brave the open ocean to traverse from the last small island up to Eriskay, the swells grew and the wind whipped around us.

At one point in the night, we heard the sound of an engine over the waves and were terrified that a ship would come bearing down on us without ever seeing us in the water. We frantically searched for their running lights, but quickly remembered that because of the restrictions, any ship would either be a warship, the Coast Guard, or unauthorized like we were. They would most likely be running without lights.

Hamish and I argued whether or not we should turn on our flashlights so as not to be run over. But as we were yelling at each other over the sound of the wind and the noise of the engine, Hamish saw lights in the sky. We both looked up and realized that the noise was coming from a low flying plane, not another vessel. I don't know if it was a friendly or an enemy plane, but it was such a relief to know we weren't in imminent danger of being capsized.

When we arrived, the locals here recognized Hamish and quickly helped us tie up the boat. They brought us inside and rallied together to find dry clothes and warm blankets. I was shivering so badly I could barely hold on to my cup of tea. I hope my handwriting is legible, because even now I feel like my hand is shaking uncontrollably.

The journey seems to have paid off, however. As soon as our teeth stopped chattering, Hamish explained why we had come, and one of the locals ran off to fetch the radio operator. Our arrival was such an event that half the village was already there crammed into the little room. The radio operator, Angus, had clearly been awakened, for his hair was all askew and there was sleep in his eyes. But as soon as we told him who we were, he grew excited.

It turns out that the plane we saw overhead was indeed a friendly and had sent out a radio message to the islands. In it, the pilot had sent out the description of a man missing since the night of the U-Boat attack with a request to relay the message throughout the islands. Angus pulled a scrap of paper from his pants pocket and read the missing man's description to the crowd.

I can tell you; it was a surreal feeling listening to someone describe me to a tee. As he read it, the crowd grew silent, and everyone turned to stare at me. They already knew I wasn't an islander from the way I talked, but I watched as each person realized that Angus was describing me. When he finished, the crowd was completely silent.

I finally broke the silence. I don't remember exactly what I said, but it was something to the effect of, "It appears as though I have been found." The crowd erupted in questions and excitement.

Eventually I was able to quiet everyone down so that I could pose the question we had braved the seas to ask. Did Angus' radio have a strong enough signal to reach Oban?

His answer almost destroyed me. No. Only the radio on Barra had a strong enough signal to reach that far.

My heart felt like that little boat being swept up and down giant swells of emotion. In one second, I had hope I could let you know I was alive and trying to reach you. In the next, my hopes were dashed. Angus tried to comfort me. The pilot said he would return as soon as he could and would await our response. But who knows when that will be? Do they patrol the islands once a week? Once a month? I imagine the squadron is stretched so thin that they don't have the manpower to be everywhere all of the time. Even the islanders said they couldn't remember the last time an aerial patrol had passed overhead.

No, if I am to return to you by Christmas, it is up to me to make it happen. Whether Hamish and I make a run for the mainland in his little boat or we find someone else willing to take us, I will find a way to return to you. I swear to you that I will do everything in my power. Wait for me, my sweet Adeline. I am coming.

Yours forever,

George

Chapter 7

ADELINE

Dear George,

I don't think I can take the ups and downs any longer. I am to the point that I just need to know. Are you there? Are you fighting to return to me?

I heard back from the pilot who flew the patrol flight over the Hebrides. He reported that he was successfully able to broadcast your description and received at least one reply in acknowledgment. He was then heading south to cover the last island when he saw a small boat or foreign object in the water, so he had to change course and report his finding to the Royal Navy.

I've listened every evening to the BBC and haven't heard any news on what it may have been or what they found.

He, of course, was restricted from telling us anything further.

I find my imagination wandering often as we get closer to my self-imposed deadline of Christmas. I have had repeated dreams about what might have happened to you. In one, you were rescued from the sea and have been convalescing in some remote monastery or something. In another, you have amnesia and don't remember who you are. In yet another, this one more of a nightmare, you were picked up by the Germans and are being held prisoner aboard their U-Boat.

I have one recurring dream where the ship is going down and your foot gets tangled in a length of rope. You are screaming for me to come and help you get free as the water rises up around you. I always wake up in a sweat just as the icy water reaches your chin. One night I must have screamed, because Mildred came rushing into my room to ask what was the matter. She spent the rest of the night laying by my side and consoling me until I finally fell asleep.

When I'm helping Mildred in the shop, my mind often wanders. When someone enters the shop, and the little bell above the door rings, my heart skips a beat and I look up in hopes of seeing you standing there in the doorway. Logically, I know it isn't you, but my heart doesn't seem to understand.

I'm even starting to see you. Yesterday I went out to the shops to buy bread. I saw a man turn the corner, and for some irrational reason, I was convinced it was you. I chased after him, calling your name. When I turned the corner, I almost ran right into him. It was just the grocer arranging apples in their display case. I can only imagine the look of disappointment on my face when I realized it wasn't you. The grocer seemed very concerned and asked if I needed a doctor. The townspeople have been very gracious and patient with me, but I'm afraid that they may think I'm cracking up.

Tonight is Christmas Eve, and the town is hosting a Christmas Cèilidh in the White Hart pub on the High Street. Mildred told me that it is an annual tradition, and everyone in town will be there. Of course, this year will be different with many of the men away to war. She invited me to come but I'm not sure I can put on a smile or be very good company. Mildred reminded me that she would be there without her husband as well, as would many other women. But everyone is determined to boost each other's spirits and enjoy Christmas. I couldn't refuse.

She was kind, but I couldn't help but feel that she was gently reminding me that I am not the only woman in town who has or will lose their husband in this war. We need each other; we need to stick together and give each other strength. I felt reproached and humbled at her reminder.

I'm afraid I have become selfish in my grief. My mother taught me better than that.

I remember a Christmas when I was probably eleven or twelve. There was a girl in my class at school named Emilee. I will never forget her. She was as timid as a mouse. Her clothes were ragged and faded, but always scrubbed clean. She never raised her hand in class, and when the teacher called on her, you could barely hear her speak.

My desk was next to hers, and I frequently had to nudge her awake when her forehead fell to the desktop. I've never known another child who was as exhausted as she was all of the time. She was skinny and frail and had dark circles under her eyes. I don't believe I ever saw her smile. She kept her head down and spoke to no one.

You can imagine how the other children teased her incessantly. I'm ashamed to admit that I joined in and laughed with them. I never made the jokes, but I never stood up for her either.

One day, I went home and asked my mom about Emilee's family. I remember it very clearly. We were standing in the kitchen and my mom was filling a basket with canned preserves, fresh bread, eggs, and a package from the corner butcher's shop. The kitchen was warm and smelled of freshly baked bread. I know it was close to Christmas because I remember how excited I was to trim the tree when my dad got home from work.

"Do you mean Emilee Duncan?" she asked me. "How do you know her?"

I explained that Emilee sat next to me in class and that her clothes were old, and she was always tired. My mom pushed the basket to the center of the table and sat down. She took my hands in hers and told me the basket she was preparing was actually meant for the Duncans. Emilee's father had been crippled in a factory accident and could no longer work. Her mom did laundry and Emilee had to wake up early every morning to collect dirty laundry from all of their clients before school. Then she stayed up late every night to help her mom fold the clothes and return them. They barely made enough to live.

I broke into tears and confessed how I had laughed when the other children teased Emilee at school. I felt so ashamed. My mom pulled me into a hug and instead of chiding me, asked me what I thought I should do. She gently wiped away my tears with the hem of her apron. I suddenly had an idea and ran to my room. I brought back one of my dresses, my old coat that didn't fit me so well anymore, and one of my favorite dolls. My mom asked if I was sure, and I nodded eagerly. So, she helped me to wrap the presents and we went together to deliver the basket to the Duncan family.

I will never forget the look on Emilee's face when she opened the presents. It was the best feeling I had ever felt, and I committed then and there to always help people no matter what their circumstances. My mom taught me that. I can't say I have always kept that commitment. I can still be selfish at times. But Mildred reminded me of that again today. It does no good for me to wallow in self-pity when there are others out there who could use my help.

So, that will be my Christmas promise this year, despite what happens between us. I will renew the promise that I made as an eleven-year-old girl.

Speaking of parents, I have avoided writing about yours but can't anymore. When I explained to them that I had to stay until Christmas, they at first tried to convince me that I was being unreasonable. Your mother just said that she couldn't spend another day in this place because it reminded her of you. Your father told me I was being silly and irrational. "He is either dead or alive, and Christmas has nothing to do with it," he said. They gave me an ultimatum. I could return to Edinburgh with them the next day or I was on my own.

I was devastated. I refused to grovel even though I desperately need their support. They are the only other people who know you, who know what I have lost. We should be strengthening each other. True to their word, they left the next day on the bus. Your father shook my hand rather formally, but your mother gave me a hug and whispered that I was welcome any time. She slipped a train ticket into my pocket, which I only discovered later that afternoon.

I am trying to be understanding and to not judge your parents too harshly. They are grieving in their own way as well and deserve my grace. I know that things would have been much different had you and I showed up at their home, hand in hand, and surprised them with the news of our marriage. Everything could have been different.

I just know that you're out there. You aren't going to receive this letter, but I want you to know that tomorrow morning I will be standing out at the harbor watching for a boat to appear on the horizon. I will be there waiting for my Christmas miracle.

I love you with my whole heart,

Adeline

Chapter 8

GEORGE

Adeline My Love,

A lot has happened since we arrived here in Lochboisdale. I have spent the majority of my time planning and preparing for what we are about to do. Let me explain. Hamish's little boat is much too small to try and make it to the mainland. We've studied every possible route and have decided that we must sail towards the isles of Canna and Rum and then south into the Inner Seas. There is no way to avoid the open ocean.

I was despairing that we would never find a way when the local tavern keeper introduced us to a man who will not give us his real name. He just has us call him "Mac." He owns a fishing trawler and has been making runs to the mainland regularly since the restrictions were put in place. Technically, what he is doing is illegal, but he says his ancestors didn't cower in port whenever there was a threat, and he wouldn't either.

Mac has offered to take me on as a passenger for his run tonight. He has a hold full of fish he wants to get to Oban in time for Christmas. One of his crew is injured, so when he heard we were trying to find passage, he thought we could help. I believe he was disappointed when he learned that I am not an experienced sailor, but Hamish volunteered to come along as well to take the crewman's place. I've been ordered to stay below out of the way.

It gets dark so early this time of year, so we'll set sail at dusk. By the time we reach open water it should be dark. I am being called to help load fish onto the boat, so I will try and finish my letter during the voyage.

We managed to leave the harbor unseen and so far, have not been caught by patrols. The night is pitch black and the men all work in silence. They know their tasks so well that there is no need to speak. I am sitting down in the cabin being rocked by the ocean swells and creak of the boat. The smell of fish permeates the room and I'm afraid it does my clothes as well. I long to be out on deck in the fresh air, but Mac has forbidden it. He says I will only get in the way as they work in darkness.

With nothing else to do but write, my mind wanders back to Christmas Eve's past. We would always attend church services on Christmas Eve.

Although I was just a boy, I always enjoyed going to church, especially the Christmas Eve service. The sound of the organ accompanying the choir as they sang Christmas hymns was magical to me. The music filled every corner of the old stone church until it reverberated in my chest. I've never felt anything like it since.

I remember one particular Christmas Eve when I was very young. I could barely see over the pew in front of me, so my view was completely blocked when a man in a tan wool coat sat down. It's funny that I can recall that mundane detail. Anyway, I was fidgeting and distracted in my seat like any little boy would be when the vicar finished his sermon and the organ hit the first chord of Joy to the World. I was so startled that I cried out. "What was that noise, Mommy?" Everyone in the congregation heard and many giggled. My mother was mortified. She put her gloved hand over my mouth and shushed me. That was when the choir joined in, and I was just riveted. I climbed up and stood on the pew so that I could see over the man's head, and according to my mother, I stared open mouthed at them throughout the entire song.

As the song ended, the church bells began to ring. It was midnight—Christmas Day. Oh, that was so magical. I can't wait to take you there so that you can hear the bells ring as well. It is one of my favorite sounds in the world.

                              Something's happened. I'll be back.

I'm back, and you won't believe me. As I was sitting there writing to you and recalling the Christmas bells, there was a horrible screech across the hull and I was thrown against the table with great force. The boat came to a sudden stop and all of the men topside began yelling. After sailing in silence for so long, the noise was jarring in the night.

I ran up to the deck to see what happened but it was so dark it took my eyes time to adjust. As shadows and shapes came into focus, I could see the rounded shape of something off the port side. I ran to the rail to look over.

At first I thought that we must have hit a whale or some other giant sea creature, but suddenly a spotlight swept over our boat. My heart sank. Had we been caught by a coastal patrol? But the truth was even more unbelievable than that. They shone the light right in my eyes, blinding me and disorienting me in the darkness. I had to grab onto the rail to steady myself.

It was then that I noticed the voices. Men were yelling across the water, but I couldn't understand what they were saying. I was so confused at our circumstances that it took me a moment to realize that the language I was hearing was German!

My eyes readjusted to the night and the vessel came into view, black against the roiling waves. I couldn't believe my eyes. I pointed dumbly, unable to speak at first. Hamish joined me at the rail and just whistled. You have probably guessed by now, but it was the German U-Boat and our vessel had tried to sail right over the top of it. We had "run aground" on a submarine.

The spotlight operator moved the light across the waves, then suddenly stopped when it found something in the water. The Germans began yelling and pointing. I looked closer and realised in horror that it was a man. The collision must have thrown him from the conning tower. His dark uniform made him difficult to spot, but I could see him struggling to stay afloat. My mind instantly went back to my ordeal in the freezing sea and my first thought was that he deserved his fate. I felt no pity that he was experiencing that which he had done to me.

But then guilt washed over me. Yes, he is our enemy, but he is also just a man. He probably has a family back home who pray for his safe return. He is one of God's children despite everything. It's Christmas Eve after all. Couldn't we set aside the war and my desire for revenge for a moment on Christmas? I rebuked myself and jumped into action.

The current was sweeping him away from the conning tower of the submarine towards us. I found the boat's life preserver and threw it into the sea. My first throw was pitiful and I had to reel the preserver back aboard to try three more times until I managed to land the preserver close enough for him to grab onto. We pulled him in and immediately got him out of his sodden clothes and under a pile of wool blankets. As he shivered under the blankets, I had flashbacks of me being in almost the same position. They were memories I didn't realize I had. I must say it was an inopportune time for me to start remembering.

It wasn't until I was setting his uniform to the side that I realized that he was not any old sailor. I'm no expert in Nazi rank insignia, but I could tell that he was an officer of some sort. The men on the submarine held the spotlight on us and watched as we cared for their officer.

Mac forced some hot coffee down the man's throat with a nip of whiskey I'm sure. He came to and began coughing.

It took him a moment to realize that he was not on his submarine with his men and he recoiled when he realized we were speaking English.

None of us could speak German, but he was luckily able to speak a little bit of English, although it was difficult to understand over the sound of his chattering teeth. As he was trying to explain who he was, someone on the U-Boat found a bullhorn and began making demands that we return their captain immediately or they would fire on us.

Their captain! We just captured the captain of the U-Boat our forces have been searching for for weeks. Can you believe it? The man on the bullhorn sounded more worried than threatening, but we were certain that they wouldn't actually shoot at us while we had their captain aboard.

Now we must decide what to do. We have brought the captain below where it is warmer and have been arguing for the last twenty minutes on whether we should make a radio call to the Coast Guard. Technically, we are not supposed to be here, but can they really prosecute us when we will be heroes for capturing a German U-Boat?

I finally stepped aside and am focusing on writing to you while Hamish and Mac continue to argue. I've said my peace. I believe we have to report it.

Well, they have finally stopped arguing and Mac has gone to the bridge. He finally decided that turning over the U-Boat is more important than his cargo of fish.

He's back and has reported that there is a Navy patrol vessel within an hour of our position. We have been instructed to stand fast and attempt to keep the U-Boat on the surface until they arrive. I am going to help bring the captain topside to reassure his crew that he is well. We have to keep our line of communication open. Now that we have broken radio silence anyway, we can try to get the submarine on the radio.

As if this night has not been exciting enough, the story continues! As soon as we got topside, the captain began yelling at his crew in German. I'm not sure, but I think he knows that we called for help and he was ordering them to submerge. We had to hold him down and gag him. Luckily, I don't think that they heard him over the waves.

We were able to establish radio contact with the U-Boat, and they found a crew member who speaks English. As we waited very impatiently for the naval vessel to arrive, we pretended to negotiate the Captain's return. The situation got a bit dicey at one point. As we were communicating over the radio, the Germans launched a small boat in secret. It wasn't until they suddenly moved the spotlight from where the Captain was restrained on the deck into our eyes that we knew something was amiss.

Hamish saw the inflatable boat first, just as it was about to reach us. I was still blinded by the light. He leapt into action, grabbing the captain by the shoulders and pointing a gun to his head. I was stunned. I had no idea where he got the gun or what was going on.

But he pushed the stumbling prisoner to the rail and shouted at the raiding party below to back off or he would shoot. There was a moment of tense silence before they thought better of it and backed away.

They stayed in the water, just out of the circle of light, waiting for us to let our guard down.

The Navy finally arrived. Even though I knew they were coming, they still surprised me. At one moment, the sea was empty; in the next, the entire world lit up around us. The Germans who were still on the conning tower panicked and scrambled below. As the Navy gave orders for them to surrender, the submarine suddenly began to sink below the waves, freeing our boat. The raiding party in the inflatable watched in horror as they were left behind.

I will never be able to forget what happened next. A klaxon sounded and depth charges rolled from racks at the stern of the warship. As soon as our boat broke free, Mac gunned the engine away from the attack. Seconds later, great columns of water exploded into the air. As we circled the warship, I saw debris float to the surface. The U-Boat captain watched in horror, knowing his vessel had been destroyed and his men sent to the bottom of the sea.

A team from the warship boarded us and took control of the captain and the raiding party in the inflatable. They said nothing about us ignoring the restrictions, which I for some reason found hilarious in the moment, probably a result of stress. But, they wished us a safe passage and just sailed away. I don't think they want to admit that a mere fishing trawler did what they have been trying to do for weeks.

I think I am finally beginning to calm down from the night's excitement. We are in the Inner Seas now, and Mac said we will arrive in Oban at daybreak. I am going to try and sleep a bit, although I don't know if that will be possible.

Dawn is breaking and I am sitting on deck waiting for the sun to rise. We just passed a lighthouse on our starboard side, and I can just make out buildings in the distance through the fog.

The sun has finally peeked over the hills, and I am soaking in its warmth. I am so nervous to finally hold you in my arms that I am keeping busy by continuing to write. Forgive me if I am not making sense.

I can see the High Street now and the other boats docked in the harbor. We are sailing into the sun, but the town is still in shadow.

There is the kirk. Its bells are ringing in Christmas morning. It's the exact sound I remember from my youth—the sound of Christmas.

People have begun to gather at the docks. Has word already spread of our exploits or are they just surprised to see a vessel so blatantly disregarding the restrictions? I am frantically searching the crowd for your face.

Away from the crowd, someone stands alone. Could it be? Is that you, my darling? Did you wait for me? Did you also pray for a Christmas miracle?

It is! I can see you clearly now. It is you! I am coming to you. I am here. I am finally here.

Merry Christmas my love,

George

A Letter From Marcus

Dear Reader,

I want to say a huge thank you for choosing to read *The Wee Christmas Letters*. If you enjoyed it and want to keep up-to-date with all of my latest releases, just sign up at the link outlined below. If you enjoyed this story, please check out my other books.

In the meantime, if you loved *The Wee Christmas Letters*, I would be enormously grateful if you would write a review. I'd love to hear what you think, and it makes such a difference helping new readers to discover one of my books for the first time.

I love hearing from my readers—you can get in touch on my Facebook page, @marcuswilliamsauthor, TikTok, X, or my website. Sign-up for my newsletter to receive a free e-book, keep in touch, and be the first to hear about new projects and upcoming books.

Thanks,

Marcus Williams

https://books.marcuswilliamsauthor.com/